The 108th Sheep

For all who cannot sleep.

–A. I.

tiger tales
an imprint of ME Media, LLC
202 Old Ridgefield Road, Wilton, CT 06897
First published in the United States 2007
Originally published in Great Britain 2006
by Cat's Pyjamas
an imprint of Fernleigh Books
Text copyright ©2006 Ayano Imai/Fernleigh Books
Illustrations copyright ©2006 Ayano Imai
CIP Data is available
ISBN-13: 978-1-58925-063-5
ISBN-10: 1-58925-063-X
Printed in Belgium
All rights reserved
1 3 5 7 9 10 8 6 4 2

The 108th Sheep

by Ayano Imai

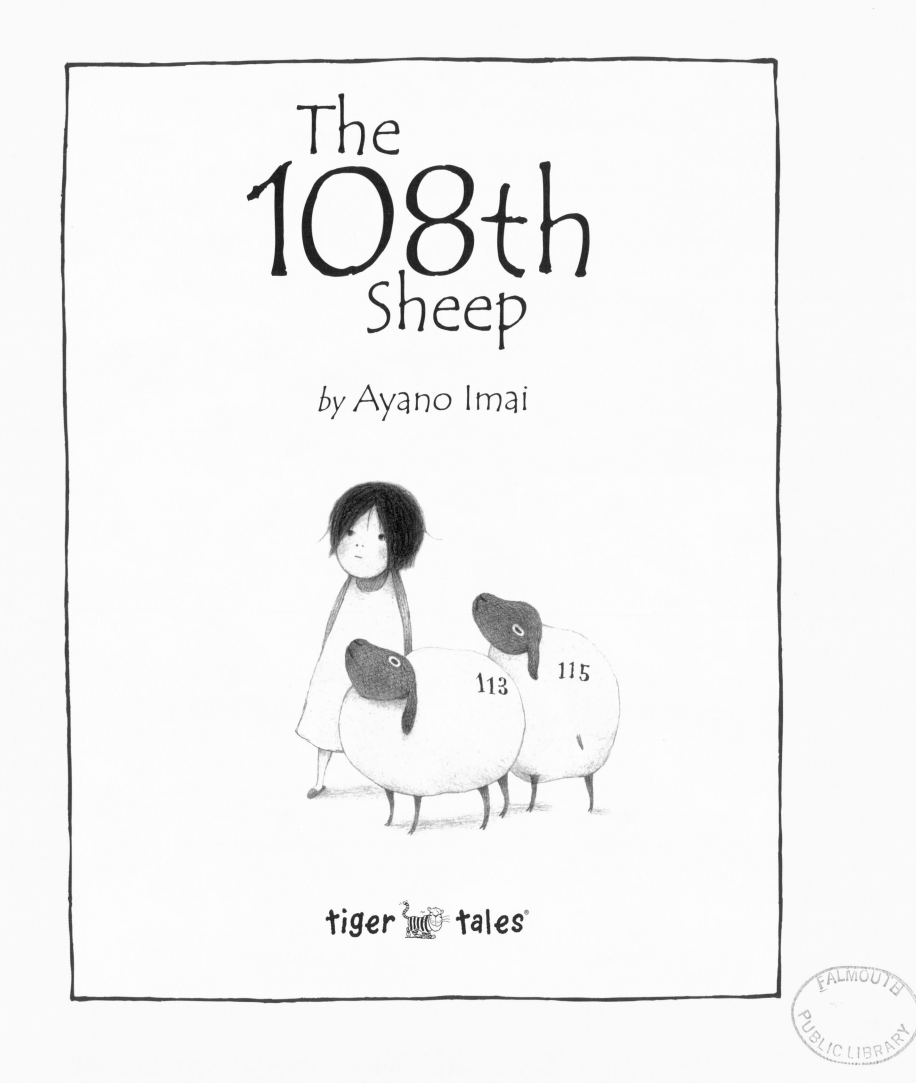

tiger tales

Emma couldn't sleep a wink.
    She tried everything she could think
of, but nothing made her sleepy.
    She drank warm milk . . .

and read lots of books. But they only made her feel more awake.

Then she had the perfect idea.

"I'll count sheep!" she thought. "That will make me fall asleep. By the time I count to ten, I'll be nodding off!"

So Emma couldn't believe it when she counted 100 sheep and was still going.

"There goes 106," she said. "And there's 107. And now here comes . . ."

There was a thud, and Emma's bed shook slightly.

The 108th sheep did not appear.

Emma quietly stepped out of bed
to see what was wrong. Behind the
headboard, she found the 108th sheep
flat on the floor with a bump on
its forehead.

"I can't do it!" he bleated.

"I've been training hard like all the other sheep," he whimpered, "but I never could jump very high. And I certainly can't jump over your bed."

And with that, the 108th sheep burst into tears.

"This is a big problem," said the 109th sheep, pushing forward. "If 108 doesn't jump over your bed, Emma, then none of us can get any sleep. And we're so tired!"

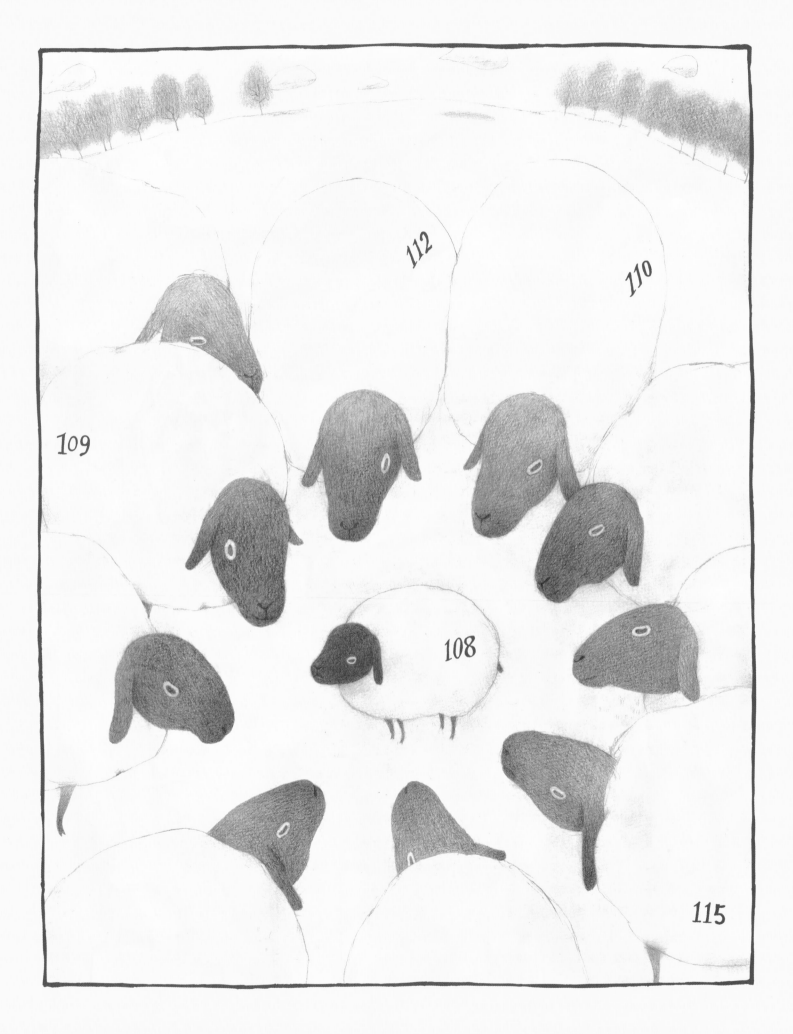

"Well," cried Emma, "then we must help 108 find a way to jump higher!" So she and the sheep tried one idea and another and another. . . .

But nothing seemed to help the 108th sheep.

"There's only one thing left to do,"
said Emma, and she began to cut a large
hole in the headboard.

All the sheep, from 109 to infinity,
held their breath as the 108th sheep
took a running jump. Up, up he soared,
bleating hopefully as he went.

Down, down toward the hole
he flew...

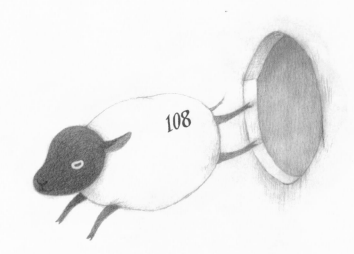

and slipped through and landed safely
on the other side!

At last, everyone curled up and
fell asleep.

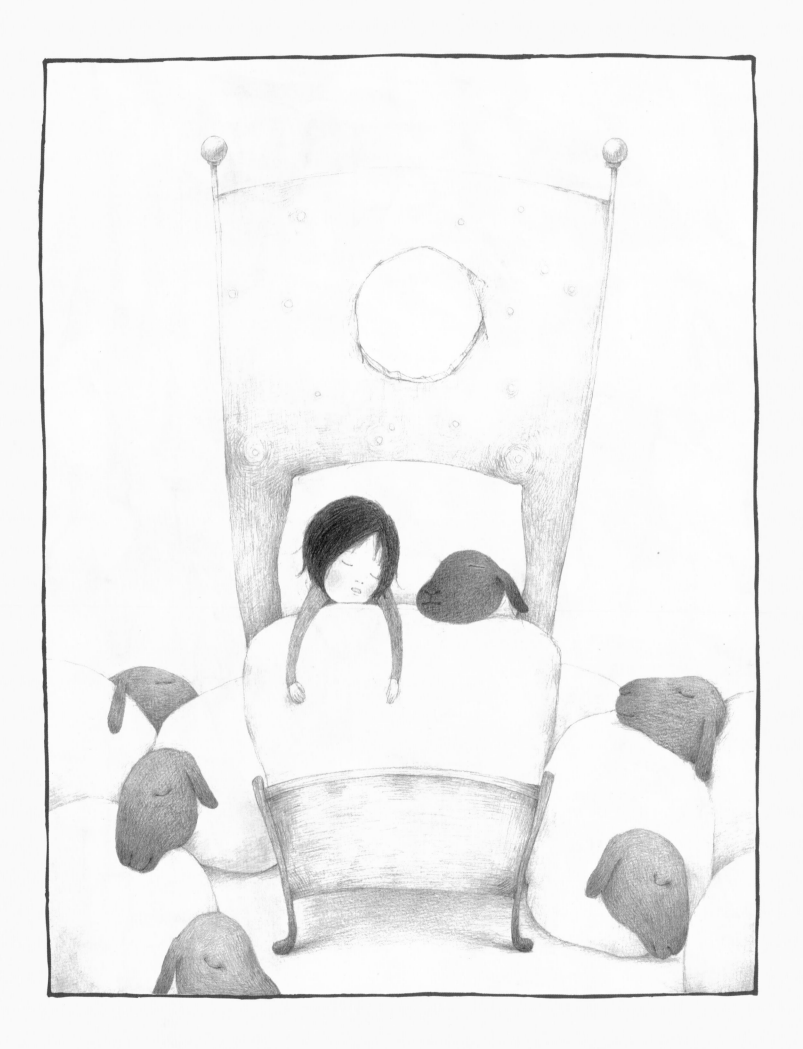

Emma awoke the next morning after a
wonderful, peaceful sleep. The hole in the
headboard was gone. The sheep in her bed
were gone, too.

"I think I will always sleep well from
now on," she said, smiling to herself.

And the 108th sheep knew that she
was right.